HOW TO LIVE
LIKE A KING ... IN AMERICA

BY GRACE R. BOYLE

BOOK DESIGN BY SAM R. RUSSO

PHOTOGRAPHY BY PETER BOYLE

"How to Live Like a King...in America," by Grace R. Boyle. ISBN 978-1-60264-095-5.

Published 2007 by Virtualbookworm.com Publishing Inc., P.O. Box 9949, College Station, TX 77842, US.

Published in the United States of America.

Acknowledgements: Special thanks are due the New York Mets for permission to use the New York Mets logo in this publication. Special thanks also to Patricia Prentice for permission to publish photographs of her son, Jason Prentice, in this book.

STARRING

ANDY

Andy is a Cavalier King Charles Spaniel owned by Mr. and Mrs. Peter Boyle, La Quinta, California. Born in 2001, Andy likes best to take long walks and sit on laps. Andy's Breeder: Bailebrae Cavaliers, Lodi/Woodbridge, California.

BARNEY

Barney is a Chocolate Labrador Retriever owned by Mr. and Mrs. Armand Pedicini, La Quinta, California. Born in 2003, Barney likes best to swim and be petted. Barney's Breeder: Country Lane Labradors, Orange County, California.

HOW TO LIVE LIKE A KING*

*A CAVALIER KING CHARLES SPANIEL

FIRST,

CHOOSE
TO LIVE
IN A LAND
WHERE
YOUR HOME
IS
YOUR CASTLE...

SECOND,

HAVE
A
NAME
BEFITTING
OF
YOUR
HERITAGE

BAILEBRAE DANDY ANDREW THE ROYAL RASCAL OF BRAMBLESHIRE

"BUT
YOU CAN
CALL
ME
ANDY"

LIKE IN
YANKEE DOODLE
D'ANDY

Mind the music and the step
And with the girls be handy

"I am that Yankee Doodle Boy!"

THIRD,

MAKE
FRIENDS
WITH A
CHOCOLATE
LAB

HE'S BIG,
HE'LL
WATCH
OVER
YOU

HE'S LOYAL,

HE'LL
ALWAYS BE THERE
TO
PROTECT
YOU

HE'S ALL AMERICAN

For it's one, two, three strikes, you're out

TRY
NOT
TO
LAUGH...

IF YOUR
CHOCOLATE
LAB
FRIEND
LOOKS LIKE
A CHOCOLATE
BAR

FOURTH,

WIN THE HEARTS OF YOUR SUBJECTS

POUR ON THE CHARM!

remember me to Herald Square

Tell all the gang at Forty Second street ♫

Oh give my regards to old Broadway

FIFTH,

TAKE
ADVANTAGE
OF YOUR
HIGH PLACED
CONNECTIONS

♪ "I want to be there when the band starts playing" ♫

HOBNOB WITH CELEBRITIES

SIXTH,

BE AMERICAN !

BE ADVENTUROUS !

SEVENTH,

ALWAYS
AND ALWAYS
SHOW
HOW PROUD
YOU ARE
OF
AMERICA

EIGHTH,

AND
ALWAYS
AND ALWAYS
TREAT YOUR
FRIENDS
AS
EQUALS

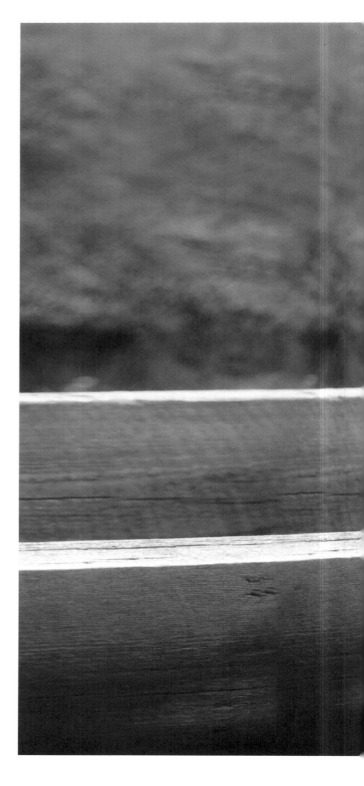

An all 'round good fellow, is my old pal ♪♪

BECAUSE,
AS
EVERYONE KNOWS,
YOU DON'T
HAVE TO BE
A KING
TO LIVE LIKE A KING
...IN AMERICA

Hail! Hail!

The gang's all here

WHO'S WHO

GRACE R. BOYLE

Grace R. Boyle's writing career has run the gamut from newspaper reporting, to advertising copywriting, to technical writing. A graduate of Niagara University, New York, she was a newspaper editor and owner/creative director of an advertising agency. Grace presently does freelance writing work from her home office in La Quinta, California. The idea for this book came about because she wanted to "say something positive about America." She chose to feature her dog Andy because of his upbeat personality and "that face."

SAM R. RUSSO

Sam R. Russo, a graduate of State University of New York at Buffalo and the Albright-Knox Art School, is an artist of international recognition. His work is in permanent collections including among others the Albright-Knox Art Gallery, Buffalo; Betty Parsons Collection, New York City; James D. Fleck Collection, Toronto; Burchfield-Penney Art Center, Buffalo; and Ball State University Gallery, Muncie, Indiana. Sam is currently exploring the artistic capabilities of today's computers. He designed this book using digital photo editing software. Sam resides in Toronto.

PETER BOYLE

Peter Boyle's love of photography has accompanied him in his travels around the world during his career as a petroleum engineer. A graduate of the University of Southern California, Peter's profession has taken him to foreign countries including Egypt, Pakistan, Libya, and Nigeria. His camera has gone with him and, now retired, his love of photography is a serious pastime. Peter resides in La Quinta, California, and Breckenridge, Colorado. The settings for many of the photos in this book are the mountain trails and wild flower meadows around Breckenridge.

Peter's photos are those of the Cavalier King Charles Spaniel and the Chocolate Labrador Retriever. Also in the book are stock photos edited and enhanced by the designer.

Printed in the United States
95740LV00002B